Promises

For J. L. M.
—E. W.

To Dilys Evans
—B. L.

A portion of the royalties from this book will be donated to Cancer Care, Inc.

Clarion Books
a Houghton Mifflin Company imprint
215 Park Avenue South, New York, NY 10003
Text copyright © 2000 by Elizabeth Winthrop
Illustrations copyright © 2000 by Betsy Lewin

Type for this book was set in 16-point Caslon.
Illustrations were executed in watercolor and pen.

Printed in the USA.

Library of Congress Cataloging-in-Publication Data

Winthrop, Elizabeth.
Promises / Elizabeth Winthrop ; illustrated by Betsy Lewin.
p.   cm.
Summary: A young girl experiences a range of emotions when her
mother undergoes treatment for cancer.
ISBN 0-395-82272-6
[1. Cancer–Fiction. 2. Mother and daughters–Fiction.]
I. Lewin, Betsy, ill. II. Title.
PZ7.W768Pr   2000
[Fic]–dc21   99-27186
CIP

LBM   10   9   8   7   6   5   4   3   2   1

Promises

by **Elizabeth Winthrop** • illustrated by **Betsy Lewin**

Clarion Books • New York

My mother is sick.
She goes to the hospital a lot.
Sometimes she goes for two days
and sometimes she goes for longer.
When Mommy leaves,
I hug her really hard.
One time she almost fell over
because I hugged her so tight.
She hugs me back
and whispers that she loves me
and tells me she'll be home soon.
But when she comes home,
she looks very tired
and her face looks yellow
and she goes right to bed
and stays there for a week.
I don't like what they do to her in the hospital.
Daddy says they are making her better,
but I think they're making her worse.

Today I am happy
because Mommy feels better.
I hold her hand
and we walk around the corner
and down the street with all the stores
because Mommy loves to look in the windows.

And then we turn another corner
and walk past my school and the church
and the doorman who shouts "Hi" to me.
"This is my mom," I tell him.
"We are out for a walk."
He takes off his hat and smiles at us.
We walk slowly because Mommy gets tired easily.

7

I make sure that nobody runs into her,
not the kids on skateboards
or the yappy dog that lives next door
or the delivery man with his cart.

Then I see a kid from school with his mother.
I shout, "Hey, Alan, this is my mom."
And he says "Hi" and his mom says "Hi."
But when they start to walk away,
I hear him say in a loud voice,
"Why doesn't Sarah's mom have any hair?"
I hope my mom didn't hear that,
but I think she did.
Tomorrow in school
I'm going to mash Alan's nose into his face
and then everybody will say,
"Hey, Alan, why don't you have a nose?"

By the time we get around the third corner,
Mom is happy we're almost home
because now she's really tired.
I remember when
she didn't have to go to the hospital
and she wasn't tired at all.
I remember when
she ran in a race in the park
and we all cheered and yelled
and threw paper cups of water at her.

I remember when
I didn't have to tiptoe around the house
and I could make as much noise as I wanted.

When we get home,
I go into my room and shut the door quietly.
I don't want to see Mommy's bald head right now.
I want my mother to have hair like everyone else.

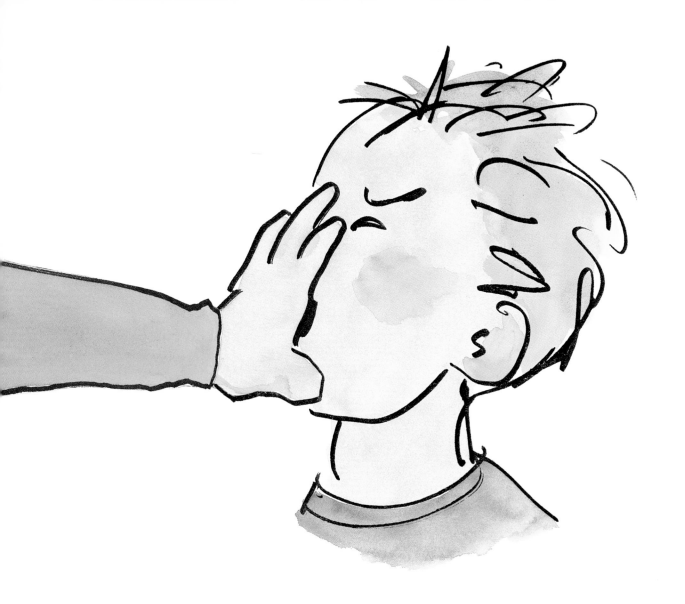

The next day when I try to mash Alan's nose in,
he cries like a baby
and Mr. Carson, the teacher,
makes me go sit in the quiet chair.
I draw a picture of my mommy,
but it doesn't look right
so I rip it up and throw it away.

"You're having a hard day, aren't you, Sarah?"
Mr. Carson says. "Is something bothering you?"
"Nothing is bothering me," I say in a loud voice.
"Especially Alan. He's not bothering me *one bit*."
"I'm glad to hear that," says Mr. Carson.

Four days later when Lucy the baby sitter
picks me up from school,
she tells me my mother had to go back to the hospital.
"She needs to have some tests," says Lucy.
She tries to hold my hand, but I don't let her.
"I have spelling tests,
but I don't have to go to the hospital," I say.
When we get home,
I run into my room and slam the door.
I jump on the bed and throw books on the floor
and turn up my music really loud.

When Daddy comes home,
he picks me up and puts me on his lap
and I don't want to cry and I'm not going to,
but then it starts and I can't stop it.
He rocks me back and forth as if I'm a baby,
but nobody's looking so I don't care.
"I want to see Mommy," I say.
"She'll be home in five days," he says.
"I want to see her *now*," I say.
Daddy gives me a hug.
"I'll talk to your mom about it tonight," he says.

The next afternoon
Daddy takes me on the bus to the hospital.
In the halls, people are rushing back and forth.
Daddy holds my hand.
We get on an elevator with people in white coats.
They are wearing little badges
with pictures of their faces.
"Are you a doctor?" I ask a lady.
"Yes, I am," she says. "Are you?"
"Nope. I'm here to see my mother," I tell her.

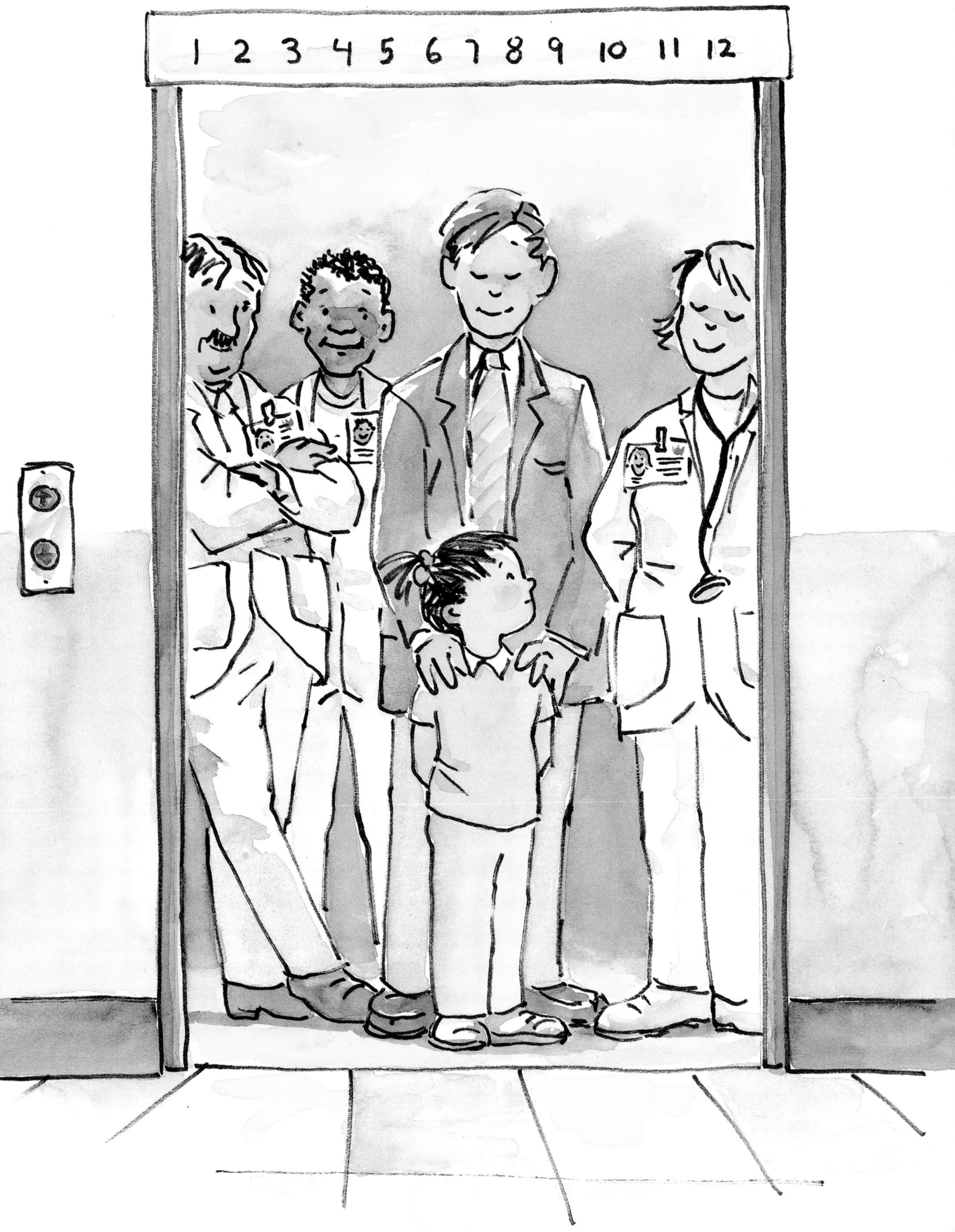
1 2 3 4 5 6 7 8 9 10 11 12

We get off on the tenth floor and go down
a long, long hallway with lots of doors.
Suddenly I don't want to see my mother.
Suddenly I'm scared that
she's going to look really funny.
Or maybe they put someone else in her bed
and hid her away somewhere
and I won't be able to find her.
I stop.
Daddy stops.
"I don't want to see her," I say. "I want to go home."
He gets down close to me.

"It's all right," he says.
"Mommy looks just the way she did last week,
except she has a pole on wheels
with a plastic bag hanging down from it
and a skinny tube running into her arm.
The medicine that's making her better
drips into the tube."
"Does the tube hurt?" I ask.
"No."
"Are you sure Mommy's still here?"
"I'm sure," he says. "Ready?"
"I guess so," I say.

So Daddy knocks on the door and pushes it open,
and there's Mommy
and she's smiling.

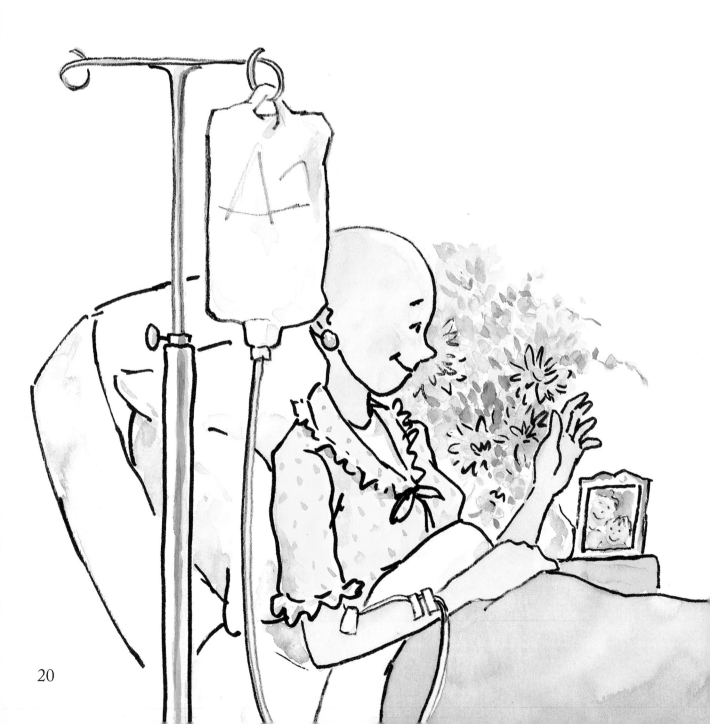

I look at the pole and the tube
and the flowers from Grandma
and the pictures of me and Daddy next to Mommy's bed.
She has a lamp
and a bell to ring for the nurse
and she has her own television
hanging from the ceiling.
"Come on up," she says.
I climb up next to her
and give her a kiss.

"People think you look funny without your hair," I say.

"I do look funny," she says.

"I don't want you to look funny," I say.

"I could get a wig," she says.

"That would look funny too," I say.

"Let's think," she says.

We lie there and we think for a long time.

"You could wear my baseball cap," I say.

"That's a good idea," she says.

"But will it fit me?"

"It has little snaps on the back
that make it bigger," I tell her.

"You can wear it until spring practice starts.
Then I need it back."

"Maybe I won't even need it that long," my mommy says.

After the visit Daddy and I go home.
We eat dinner and I give Daddy my baseball cap
so he can take it to Mommy the next day.
Then Daddy reads me a book and tucks me into bed.
"I miss Mommy," I say.
"Me too," Daddy says.
"When is she coming home?"
"Soon."
"When is soon?"
"In a day or two."
"And then she won't ever get sick again?" I ask.
"Well, she's getting a little bit better every day."
"So her hair will grow back," I say.
"And she can pick me up at school."
"That's right," Daddy says.

The day Mommy comes home,
she is wearing my Little League cap.
West Side, it says right across the front.
It looks good on her.
She wears it in bed during her resting week.

She wears it down to the lobby
the first day she collects the mail.

She wears it two weeks later
the first time she picks me up at school.
Nobody says anything funny about her hair.
She still takes a nap every afternoon
and I have to tiptoe around.
But she doesn't look yellow anymore.

Little prickly things are sticking up all over Mommy's head.
"You look like a porcupine," I say.
She laughs.
My father kisses the top of her head.
"Ouch," he says. "More like a hedgehog."
Her hair begins to grow in really fast
and it's darker than before and it's curly.
She doesn't need to wear the hat anymore,
but she wears it anyway because she likes it.
She says it keeps her head warm.

Now when she goes to the hospital,
she doesn't have to spend the night.
She comes home in the afternoon
and goes straight to bed.
The next morning
she gets up and walks me to school.
She goes for long walks
and soon she and my father start running again.
My father runs slowly so she can keep up.

The last day of school I tell Alan,
"My mom's got hair now."
And she takes off her hat and shows him.
"So what?" Alan says. "My mom's got hair too."
I burst out laughing. So does my mom.
Alan is funny.
On the way home I am happy.
"You're not going to be sick anymore," I say.
"I hope not," my mom says.
"You have to promise that you're not," I tell her.
"I can't make that promise, Sarah. I wish I could."

"Well, what can you promise?" I ask.

"I promise that I can run two miles in the park today and that we can stop for ice cream on the way home and that we'll read the book about Charlotte and Wilbur before bed tonight. Is that enough promises for today?"

"Yes," I say. "Tomorrow can we think of more?"

"Yes," my mommy says.

"Tomorrow we can think of more."